A Note to Parents and Caregivers:

Read-it! Readers are for children who are just starting on the amazing road to reading. These beautiful books support both the acquisition of reading skills and the love of books.

The PURPLE LEVEL presents basic topics and objects using high frequency words and simple language patterns.

The RED LEVEL presents familiar topics using common words and repeating sentence patterns.

The BLUE LEVEL presents new ideas using a larger vocabulary and varied sentence structure.

The YELLOW LEVEL presents more challenging ideas, a broad vocabulary, and wide variety in sentence structure.

The GREEN LEVEL presents more complex ideas, an extended vocabulary range, and expanded language structures.

The ORANGE LEVEL presents a wide range of ideas and concepts using challenging vocabulary and complex language structures.

When sharing a book with your child, read in short stretches, pausing often to talk about the pictures. Have your child turn the pages and point to the pictures and familiar words. And be sure to reread favorite stories or parts of stories.

There is no right or wrong way to share books with children. Find time to read with your child, and pass on the legacy of literacy.

Adria F. Klein, Ph.D.
Professor Emeritus
California State University
San Bernardino, California

Editor: Jacqueline A. Wolfe
Page Production: Amy Bailey Muehlenhardt
Creative Director: Keith Griffin
Editorial Director: Carol Jones
Managing Editor: Catherine Neitge
The illustrations in this book were created with watercolor and colored pencil.

Picture Window Books
A Capstone Imprint
151 Good Counsel Drive
P.O. Box 669
Mankato, MN 56002-0669
877-845-8392
www.capstonepub.com

Printed in the United States of America in Stevens Point, Wisconsin.
032013
007284R

Library of Congress Cataloging-in-Publication Data
Klein, Adria F.
Max goes to school / by Adria F. Klein ; illustrated by Mernie Gallagher-Cole.
p. cm.—(Read-it! readers)
Summary: During his day at school, Max listens to and writes a story, plays on
the playground, and eats lunch.
ISBN-13: 978-1-4048-1179-9 (hardcover)
ISBN-10: 1-4048-1179-6 (hardcover)
ISBN-13: 978-1-4048-3059-2 (paperback)
ISBN-10: 1-4048-3059-6 (paperback)
[1. Kindergarten—Fiction. 2. Schools—Fiction.] I. Gallagher-Cole, Mernie, ill.
II. Title. III. Series.

PZ7.K678324Malm 2005
[E]—dc22   2005003787

Max
Goes to School

by Adria F. Klein
illustrated by Mernie Gallagher-Cole

Special thanks to our advisers for their expertise:

Adria F. Klein, Ph.D.
Professor Emeritus, California State University
San Bernardino, California

Susan Kesselring, M.A.
Literacy Educator
Rosemount–Apple Valley–Eagan (Minnesota) School District

PiCTURE WiNDOW BOOKS
Minneapolis, Minnesota

Max likes to read and write.

Max goes to school.

He meets the teacher.

The teacher shows Max his desk.

Max sits at his desk.

The teacher reads a story.

Max listens to the story.

The teacher gives him paper,
a pencil, and a crayon.
Max draws a picture.

The teacher takes the children
to recess.

Max plays on the playground.

The teacher takes the children to lunch.

16

Max eats lunch.

The teacher says goodbye.

Max says goodbye.

Max goes home.

Max dreams of school.

Max likes to read and write.